The
Wee Christmas Cabin
of Carn-na-ween

"The Wee Christmas Cabin of Carn-na-ween," from *The Long Christmas* retold by Ruth Sawyer, copyright 1941 by Ruth Sawyer. This edition is reprinted by arrangement with Viking Children's Books, a member of Penguin Group (USA) Inc.

First Candlewick Press edition 2005

Library of Congress Cataloging-in-Publication Data

Sawyer, Ruth, 1880–1970.
The wee Christmas cabin of Carn-na-ween / Ruth Sawyer ; illustrated by Max Grafe. — 1st Candlewick Press ed.
p.   cm.
"From the Long Christmas retold by Ruth Sawyer . . . 1941"
Summary: Oona Hegarty, a poor woman, has always longed for her own cabin, and on Christmas Eve, after being trapped in the snow with no shelter, she finds a group of wee people who work to grant her wish.
ISBN 0-7636-2553-1
[1. Poor — Fiction. 2. Christmas — Fiction. 3. Fairies — Fiction. 4. Magic — Fiction. 5. Ireland — Fiction.]
I. Grafe, Max, ill. II. Sawyer, Ruth, 1880–1970. Long Christmas. III. Title
PZ8.1.S262We2005
[Fic] — dc22   2004061837

2 4 6 8 10 9 7 5 3 1

Printed in China

This book was typeset in Erasmus Light.
The illustrations were done in mixed media on paper.

Candlewick Press
2067 Massachusetts Avenue
Cambridge, Massachusetts 02140

visit us at www.candlewick.com

The
Wee Christmas Cabin
of Carn-na-ween

RUTH SAWYER

ILLUSTRATED BY MAX GRAFE

CANDLEWICK PRESS
CAMBRIDGE, MASSACHUSETTS

A hundred years ago and more, on a stretch of road that runs from the town of Donegal to Killybegs and the sea, a drove of tinkers went their way of mending pots and thieving lambs. Having a child too many for the caravan they left it, new-born, upon a cabin doorsill in Carn-na-ween.

The cabin belonged to Bridget and Conal Hegarty. Now these two had

little wish for another child, having childher aplenty of their own; but they could not leave the wee thing to die at their door, nor had they a mind to throw it into the turf-pit. So Bridget suckled it with her own wean; she divided the cradle between them. And in time she came to love it as her own and fought its battles when the neighbors would have cursed it for a tinker's child.

I am forgetting to tell you that the child was a girl and Bridget named her Oona. She grew into the prettiest, the gentlest-mannered lass in all the county. Bridget did her best to get the lads to court her, forever pointing out how clever she was with her needle, how sweet her voice when she lilted an air, the sure way she had of making bannock, broth, or jam.

But the lads would have none of her. Marry a tinker's child? Never! Their feet might be itching to take her to a cross-road's dance, their arms hungering to be holding her, but they kept the width of a cabin or the road always between her and them. Aye, there was never a chance came to Oona to marry and have childher of her own, or a cabin she could call hers.

All of Bridget's and Conal's lasses married; but Oona stayed on to mind the house for them, to care for them through their sicknesses, to help them gently into their graves. I think from the beginning Oona had a dream — a dream that, having cared lovingly for the old, someone would be leaving her at long last a cabin for her own keeping.

Bridget, before she died, broke the dream at its beginning. "The cabin goes to Michael," she said. "He and his young wife will not be wanting ye, I'm thinking. Go to the chest and take your share of the linen. Who knows but some man, losing his wife, will be glad to take ye for his second. I'd not have ye going empty-handed to him."

Oona held fast to the dream; she let neither years nor heart-aches shatter it. There was always a cabin waiting to welcome her as soon as another had finished with her. From the time when Oona left the Hegarty cabin, a bonny lass still, with strength to her body and laughter in her eyes, to the time when she was put out of the MacManuses', old and with little work left in her, the tale runs thin as gossamer. But if you are knowing Ireland and the people of Donegal it is not hard to follow the tinker's child through that running of years.

From cabin to cabin, whenever trouble or need abided, there went Oona. In a cabin where the mother was young, ailing, with her first-born, there you would find Oona caring for the child as it had been her own. In a cabin where the childher had grown and gone dandering off to Belfast, Dublin, or America and left the old ones behind, there she tended them as she would have tended her own had she ever known them. In a cabin where a man had lost his wife and was ill-fitted to mind the house and the weans

alone—aye, here she was the happiest. She would be after taking over the brood as a mother would, gentling the hurt that death had left behind, and for herself building afresh the dream.

But her birth betrayed her at every turn of the road. No man trusted her to be his first or second wife. Not one of the many she served and loved guessed of the hunger that grew with the years for a cabin she could call hers.

All blessed her name while she lived; and for the hundred years since she has been gone from Carn-na-ween the tales about her have been kept green with loving memory. Those she served saw that she never went empty-handed away. So to Bridget Hegarty's linen was added a griddle, pans, kettles, crocks, creels, and dishes.

Each thing she chose from the cabin she was leaving was something needed to make the home she dreamed of gay and hold comfort. As the years went by, the bundle of her possessions grew, even as she dwindled. Men, women, and childher who passed her on the road at such times as she might be changing cabins would stop to blather with her. Pointing to the size of her bundle they would say: "'Tis twice your size, the now. Ye'll have to be asking for oxen and a cart to fetch it away from the next cabin." And they would laugh. Or they would say: "Ye might be asking the Marquis to build ye a castle next his own. Ye'll be needing a fair-sized place to keep all ye've been gathering these many years."

Always she would blather back at them. For all her dream was dimming she was never one to get down-daunted. "Ye can never be telling," she would say, "I may yet be having a wee cabin of my own some day. I'm not saying how and I'm not saying when." And she would nod her head in a wise, knowledgeable way, as if she could look down the nose of the future and see what was there.

She was in the cabin of the MacManuses' when the great famine came. The corn in the fields blighted; the potatoes rotted in the ground. There was neither food for man nor fodder for beast. Babies starved at their mothers' breasts, strong men grew weak as childher, dragging themselves into the fields to gnaw at the blistered grass and die under a cruel, drouthing sun. Everywhere could be heard the crying of childher and the keening for the dead. At the beginning neighbor shared with neighbor until death stalked them. Then it was every cabin for itself, and many a man sat all night, fowling-piece across his knee, to keep guard over a last cow in the byre or the last measure of meal in the bin.

So old had Oona grown by famine-time that the neighbors had lost all count of her years. She moved slowly on unsteady feet. Her eyes were dulled; her speech was seldom coming now. But for all that she was worth the sheltering and the scanty food she ate. She milked, she churned, she helped the oldest lad carry the creel to the bog, she helped at the cutting of the turf. So long as there was food enough for them the MacManuses kept her and blessed the Virgin for another pair of hands to work.

But famine can put stones in the place of human hearts, and hunger can make tongues bitter. As the winter drew in, Oona for all her dullness saw the childher watching every morsel of food she put to her lips. She heard the mother's tongue sharpen as she counted out the spoonfuls of stirabout that

went into the bowls. Harvest had come and gone, and there was no harvest. The cold, cruel winds of December rattled at their doors and windows. Of one thing only was there enough: there was always turf in the bog to cut, to dry, to keep the hearth warm.

The childher in the cabin cried from cock-crow till candle-time. Oona wished her ears had been as dulled as her eyes. But for all that she closed her heart to the crying, telling herself she had earned what little food she took, and the good heat for her old body. But a night came when she could stand the crying no longer, when the spoon scraped the bottom of the meal-bin, when the last of the praties had been eaten, their skins with them.

Saying never a word she got up at last from the creepie where she had been thawing her bones and started to put together again her things into her bundle. The MacManuses watched her, and never a word said they. The corners of the great cloth were tied at last. Over her bent shoulders Oona laid her shawl. The cabin was quiet the now, the childher having cried themselves asleep with hunger. Oona dragged her bundle to the door; as she lifted the latch she spoke:

"Ye can fend for yourselves. Ye'll not want me the now."

"Aye, 'tis God's truth." It was the wife who said it.

Timothy MacManus reached for her hand: "Hush, are ye not remembering what night it is?"

"Aye, 'tis Christmas Eve. What matter? There be's not sense enough left in the old one's mind to know it. And in times such as these there is naught to put one night ahead of another."

"'Twill be a cursedes, the same, if we let her go."

"'Twill be a curse on her if she stays."

"God and Mary stay with ye, this night," Oona called, going out the door.

"God and Mary go with ye," the two mumbled back at her.

Outside Oona lifted the bundle to her back.

How she had strength for this I cannot be telling you. It often comes, a strange and great strength, to those who have borne much and have need to bear more. Oona took the road leading to Killybegs and the sea. A light snow was falling and the wind had dropped to a low whispering. As she went down the village street she stopped to glimpse each cabin and the lighted room within. Hardly a cabin but she had lived in; hardly a face but

she had read long and deeply over many years. Her lips made a blessing and a farewell for every door she passed.

All cabins were left behind as the road grew steeper. She climbed with a prayer on her lips — what prayer I do not know, but it lightened the load she carried on her back and in her heart, it smoothed the roughness of her going.

She came at last to the bogland. It stretched on and on beyond the reach of eye, even in the daylight. In the dark she sensed only a leveling off, where feet could rest. She stumbled from the road and found shelter under a blackthorn which grew on the fringe of the bog.

"I like it here," she said as she eased the bundle from her back. "Always, I have liked it here. Many's the time I have said: some day I will take the whole of it and climb the hill and sit under this very thorn, the way I'll be feeling the wind from the sea and watching the sun set on it, and the stars lighting it; and, mayhap, hearing the sound of fairy pipes. I never came; I never had the day whole."

She said it in a kind of wonder. She was safe here from the reach of neighbors. It was in her heart that she could never again bear to have man or woman offer her food needed for young mouths. Too many times she had folded tired hands; too many times she had shut weary eyes, not to know what a gentle companioning death could give the old at the end. "'Tis a friend, he is, that I have known long. 'Tis a friend he will be coming, calling softly, wishfully: 'Come, Oona!'"

After that her head grew light. She lost all count of time; she lost all track of space. She felt no cold, no tiredness. She could gather years into her mind as cards into the hand, shuffle them about and draw out the ones she liked best. She remembered suddenly that one of the reasons for wanting to climb the hill was to find the fairy rath that lay somewhere along the bog. Conall of a Thousand Songs had slept a Midsummer Night with his head to this rath and had wakened in the morning with it filled full of fairy music — music of enchantment. Wully Donoghue had crossed the rath late one May Eve and caught the fairy host riding abroad. Many a time, herself, she had put a piggin of milk with a bowl of stirabout on the back steps of those cabins she had lived in, remembering how well the Gentle People liked milk and stirabout. Aye, the Gentle People, the Good People! She hoped famine had not touched them. It would be a sorry thing to have the fairy folk starved off the earth.

She slept a little, woke, and slept again. Above the sleeping her mind moved on a slow current. Snow had covered her, warm. This was Christmas Eve, the time of the year when no one should go hungry, no one cold. It would be a white Christmas on the morrow, and the people of Donegal had a saying that when a white Christmas came the Gentle People left their raths and trooped abroad to see the wonder of it. Aye, that was a good saying. They would make good company for a lonely old woman.

Her legs were cramping under her. She strove to move them, and as she did so she had a strange feeling that she had knocked something over. Her old eyes peered into the darkness, her hand groped for whatever it was she had upset. To her amazement when she held her hand under her eyes there was a fairy man, not a hand high. His wee face was puckered with worry. "Don't ye be afeard, wee man," she clucked to him. "I didn't know ye were after being where ye were. Was there anything at all ye were wanting?"

"Aye, we were wanting ye."

"Me!"

"None else. Look!"

And then she saw the ground about her covered with hundreds upon hundreds of Gentle People, their faces no bigger round than buttons, all raised to hers, all laughing.

"What might ye be laughing at?" she asked. "Tell me, for it be's a lee long time since I had laughter on my own lips."

"We are laughing at ye, tinker's child. Living a lifetime in other folks' cabins, serving and nursing and mothering and loving, and never a cabin or kin ye could call your own."

"Aye," she sighed, "aye, 'tis the truth."

"'Tis no longer the truth. Bide where ye be, Oona Hegarty, and sleep the while."

She did as she was bidden but sleep was as thin as the snow which covered her, breaking through in this place and that, so that she might see through it what was going on about her. Hither and yon the Good People were hurrying. They brought stones, they brought turf. They laid a rooftree and thatched it. They built a chimney and put in windows. They hung a door at the front and a door at the back. As they worked they sang, and the song they made drifted into Oona's sleep and stayed with her.

'Tis a snug Christmas cabin we're building the night,

      That we're building the night.

The stones make the walls and the turf chinks it tight,

      Aye, the turf chinks it tight.

There'll be thatch for the roof to keep wind out and rain,

      To keep wind out and rain.

And a fire on the hearth to burn out all pain,

      Aye, burn out all pain.

The meal in the chest will stand up to your chin,

      Well up to your chin;

There'll be Christmas without, and Christmas within,

      Always Christmas within.

There'll be plenty of currants, and sugar, and tea,

      Aye, plenty of tea;

With the chintz at the windows as gay as can be,

      All as gay as can be.

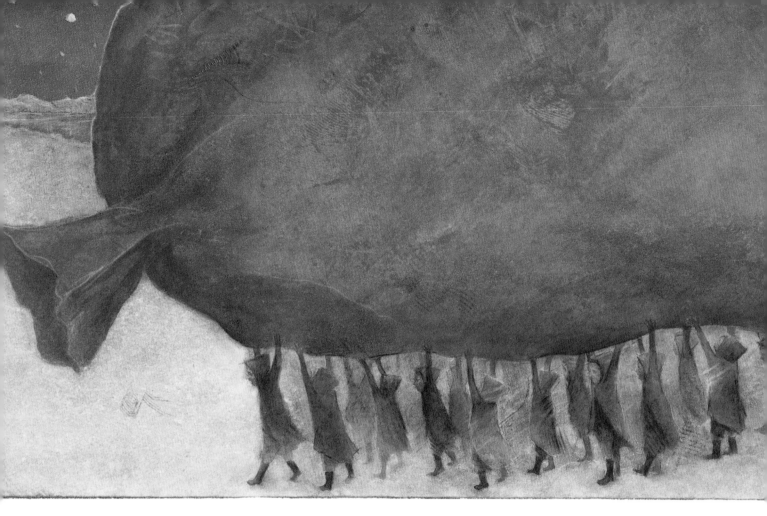

There was more to the song. It went on and on, and Oona could not tell where the song ended and the dream began, so closely woven were the two together. She felt of a sudden a small, tweaking hand on her skirt and heard a shrill voice piping: "Wake up — wake up, Oona Hegarty!"

"'Tis awake I am, entirely," said Oona, sitting up and rubbing her eyes. "Awake and dreaming at the same time, just."

"We'll be after fetching in your bundle, then; and all things shall find their rightful places at last."

Ten hundred fairy men lifted the bundle and bore it inside, with Oona following. She drew her breath through puckered lips; she let it out again in sighs of wonderment. "Is everything to your liking, ma'am?" inquired the fairy man she had knocked over.

She made the answer as she looked about her: "The bed's where it should be. The chintz now—I had a mind to have it green, with a touch of the sun

and a touch of the flaming turf in it. The dresser is convenient high. Wait till I have my bundle undone and the treasures of a lifetime put away."

The Gentle People scuttled about helping her, putting the linen in the fine oak chest, the dishes on the dresser. The kettle was hung above the hearth, the creepie put beside it. The rug spread along the bedside and the griddle left standing by the fire, ready.

All things in their right places, as the tinker's child had dreamed them.

"Is it all to your liking?" shouted the Gentle People together.

"Aye, 'tis that and more. Crocks and creels where they do belong. The fine, strong spoon to be hanging there, ready to stir the griddle-bread. The knife with the sharp edge to it, to be cutting it." She turned and looked down at the floor, at the hundreds of wee men crowding her feet: "I'm not asking why ye have done this thing for me this night. But I ask one thing more. On every white Christmas let you be bringing folk to my door — old ones not needed longer by others, children crying for their mother — a lad or a lass for whom life has gone amiss. Fetch them that I may warm them by the hearth and comfort them."

"We will do that, tinker's child; we will do that!" The voices of the Gentle People drifted away from her like a wind dying over the bog: it was there — it was gone. A great sleep took Oona Hegarty so that her eyes could stay open no longer. She put herself down on the out-shot bed. She pulled the warm blanket over her and drew the chintz curtains.

The next night — Christmas — hunger drove Maggie, the middle child of the MacManuses', out of their cabin. She went like a wee wild thing, knowing only the hunger-pain she bore and the need of staying it. Blindly she climbed the hill to the bogland. Weak and stumbling she was, whimpering like a poor, hurt creature. She stumbled off the road, she stumbled over the sudden rise on the bog which nearly laid her flat. Rubbing her eyes she looked up at a wee cabin standing where no cabin had ever been. Through the windows came a welcoming light. In wonderment she lifted the latch and went in.

"Come in, Maggie, I've been looking for ye, the lee long day." It was Oona's voice that spoke to her; aye, but what a changed Oona! She knelt by the hearth turning the griddle-bread, her eyes as blue as fairy-thimbles, her hair the color of ripened corn. There were praties boiling in the kettle, tea making on the hearth. Enough to eat and to spare. But that was not what filled the child's eyes with wonder. It was Oona herself, grown young, with the look of a young bride on her. "Take the creepie." Her voice had the low, soft calling of a throstle to its young. "Ye'll be after eating your fill, Maggie, and not knowing hunger for many a day."

And it's the truth I am telling. Maggie went back and told; but although half of Carn-na-ween hunted the cabin throughout the year none found it. Not until a white Christmas again came round. Then old Seumus MacIntyre the cobbler died, leaving his widow Molly poor and none to keep her. They were coming to fetch her to the workhouse that Christmas Eve when she took the road climbing to Killybegs and the sea, and was never seen again.

And so the tales run. There are enough to be filling a book, but why should I go on with them? You can be after telling them to yourselves. This I know: given a white Christmas this year the wee fairy cabin of Carn-na-ween will be having its latch lifted through the night by the lone and the lost and the heart-broken. Aye, Oona Hegarty, the tinker's child, will be keeping the griddle hot, the kettle full, and her arms wide to the childher of half the world this night — if it be's a white Christmas.

Glossary

BANNOCK – a type of flat, unleavened bread

CREEL – a wicker basket

CREEPIE – a low stool

OUT-SHOT BED – a sleeping nook near the kitchen hearth

PIGGIN – a small pail

PRATIES – potatoes

RATH – a circular earthwork fort built by ancient Irish chieftains; the fairy folk are said to have retreated beneath their hilly ruins and to dance nightly among them

ROOFTREE – ridgepole

STIRABOUT – a thin oatmeal porridge

TINKER – a person who travels from place to place mending metal household utensils; also used to refer to traditionally nomadic groups such as travelers or gypsies

WEAN – baby

Publisher's Note

The great famine referred to in the story is the Great Potato Famine, which struck Ireland in the 1840s. At the time, Ireland was largely divided into estates owned by English landlords and farmed by Irish tenants, who were dependent on one staple food that they grew for themselves: the potato. So when a fungus destroyed the potato crop, it caused mass hunger; hundreds of thousands died of starvation or illness. Years of land reform and political change followed, finally leading to the Republic of Ireland's independence in the early twentieth century.

The "turf" referred to in the story is peat, a naturally composted soil material found in Ireland's extensive boglands. Cut and dried in blocks, it can be burned for home cooking and heating. It can also be used as a building material, just as the fairy folk use it as mortar between the stones of Oona's cabin.